P9-DMC-562

The Contest Between the Sun and the Wind

AN AESOP'S FABLE

retold by Heather Forest   illustrated by Susan Gaber

AUGUST HOUSE
Little folk

ATLANTA

Published 2008 by August House, Inc.
augusthouse.com

Designed by Shock Design & Associates, Inc.
Printed by Pacom Korea
Seoul, South Korea
January 2013

10 9 8 7 6 5 4 3 2 1   PB

*The paper used in this publication meets the minimum
requirements of the American National Standard
for Information Sciences—Permanence of Paper
for Printed Library Materials, ANSI Z39.48-1984.*

LIBRARY OF CONGRESS CATALOGING-IN-PUBLICATION DATA

Forest, Heather.
[North Wind and the Sun]
The contest between the Sun and the Wind : an Aesop's fable / retold
by Heather Forest ; illustrated by Susan Gaber.
p. cm.
Based on a fable from Aesop, "The North Wind and the Sun."
Summary: The sun and the wind test their strength by seeing which of
them can cause a man to remove his coat, demonstrating the value
of using gentle persuasion rather than force as a means of achieving
a goal.
ISBN 978-0-87483-832-9 (hardcover : alk. paper)
ISBN 978-1-939160-66-9 (paperback)
[1. Fables. 2. Folklore.] I. Gaber, Susan, ill. II. Aesop. III. Title.

PZ8.2.F62Con 2008
398.2--dc22
[E]
2007018813

August House LittleFolk
ATLANTA

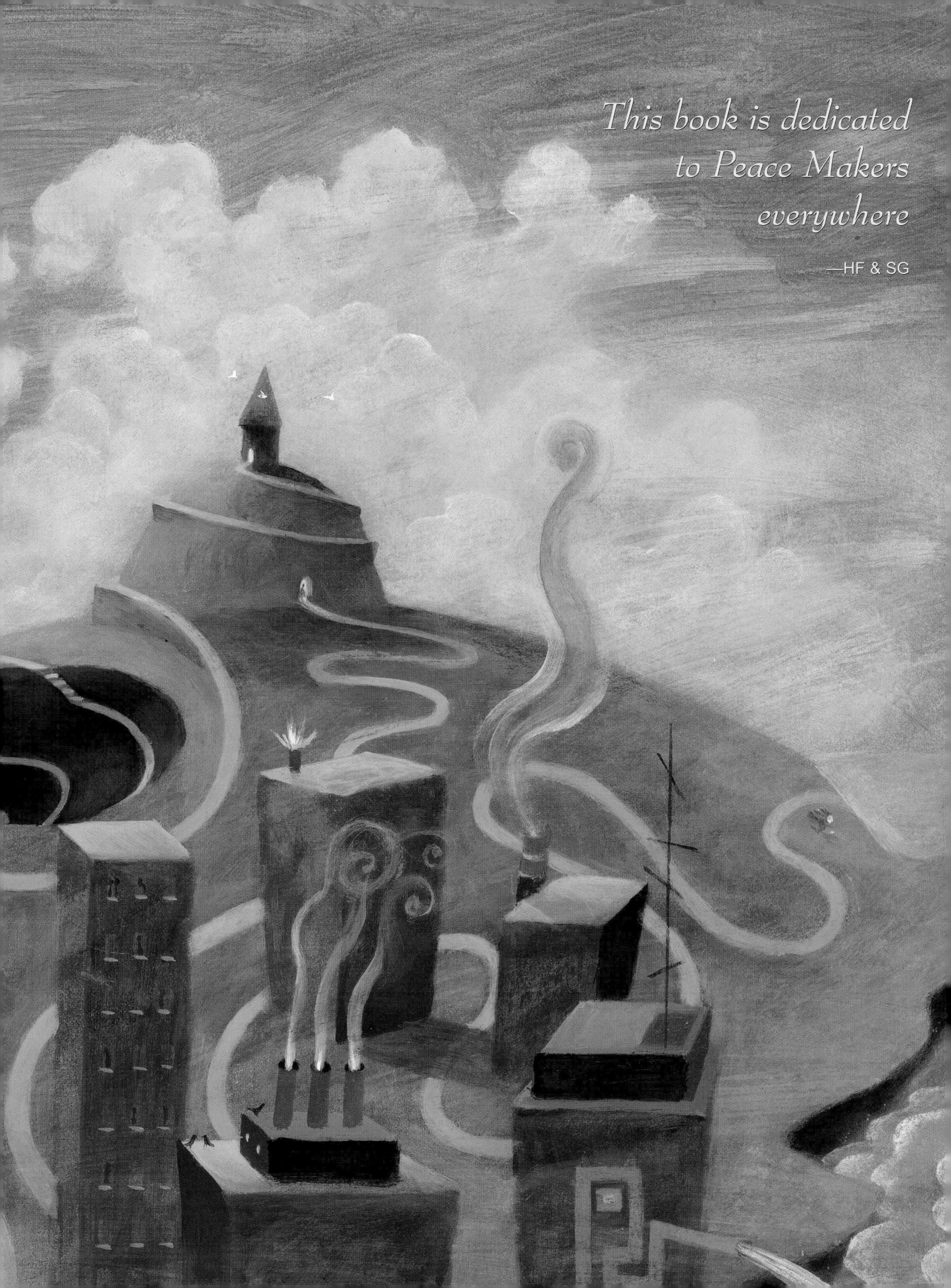

This book is dedicated
to Peace Makers
everywhere

—HF & SG

There once was a man in a warm coat,

walking his way d o w n a w i n d i n g road.

The Sun and the Wind,
high in the sky,
watched the man
as he walked by.

The Wind bragged to the Sun,
"I'm the strongest one!
I'm much stronger than you!"

"Really?" said the Sun. "Then I challenge you to a contest of strength. Let us see who can take the coat off of that man on the road."

"Oh, that's too easy!" howled the Wind.

"I'll huff and I'll puff. I'll blow to the brim. I'll RIP his coat off of him!

I'll SMASH him against the trees!

I'll take his coat off with ease!"

So. . .

The Wind blew harshly down the road.

The man clutched tightly to his coat.

The Wind grew loud.

The Wind grew cold.

The shivering man buttoned up his coat.

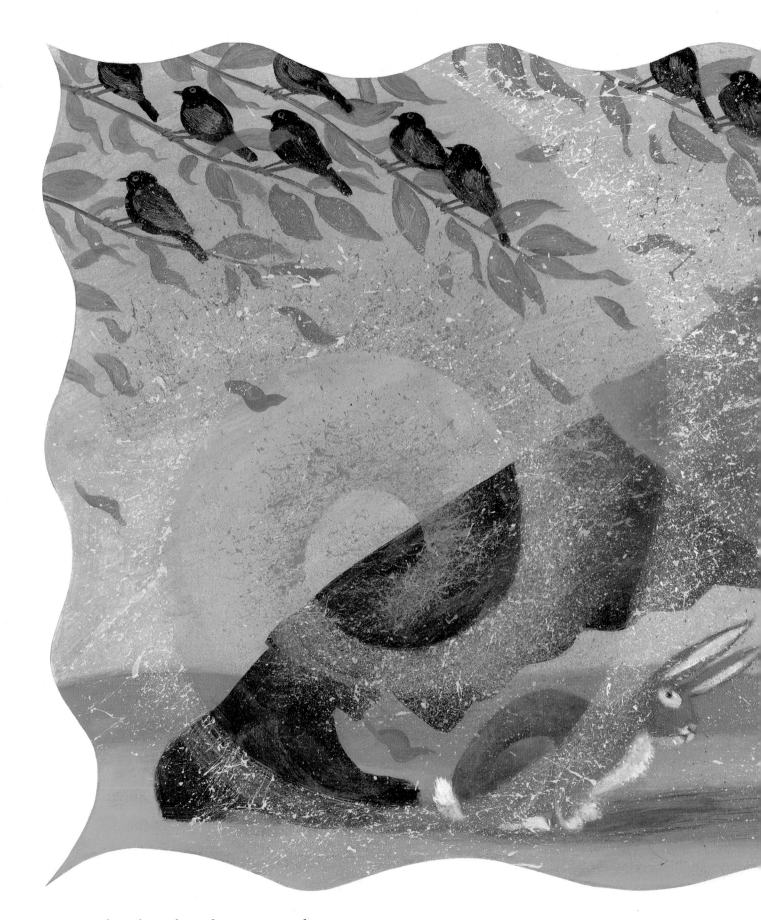

The birds clung to the trees.

The world was dust and leaves.

But the harder the Wind
blew down the road,
the tighter the man
held onto his coat.

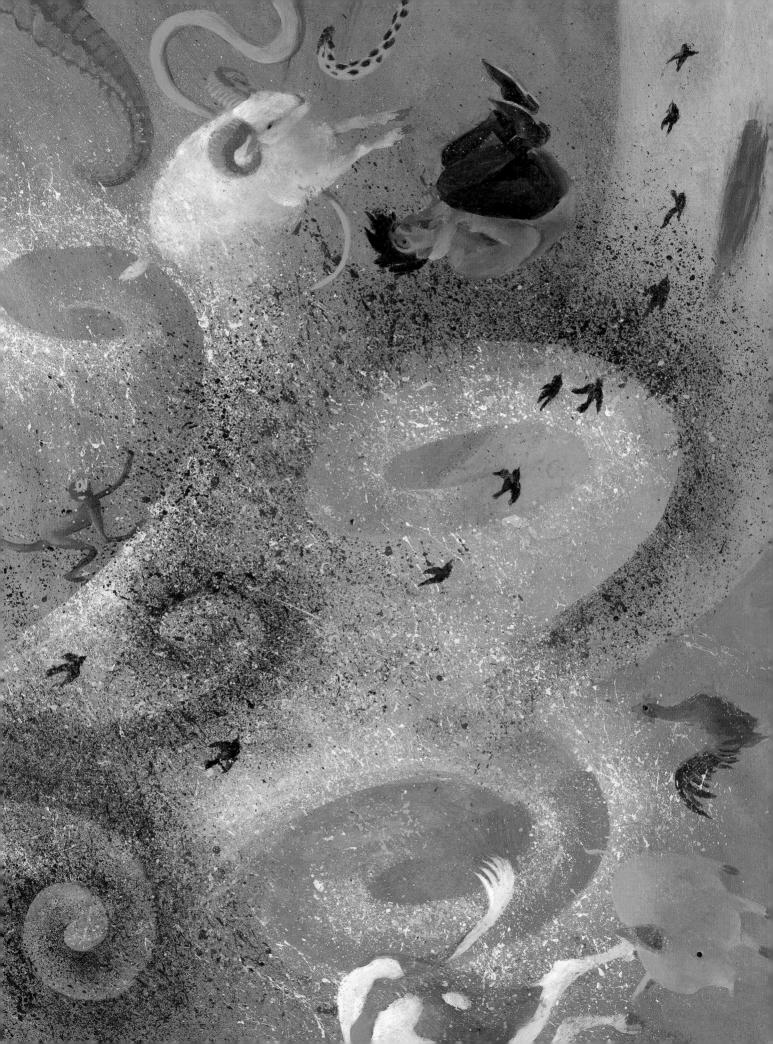

Discouraged,
the Wind blustered off
with a gust and a swirl.

Then. . .

The Sun peeked out from behind a cloud,
warming the air and the frosty ground.

The man on the road unbuttoned his coat.
He lifted his voice and sang out loud.

The Sun grew even brighter,

and brighter,

and brighter,

and brighter.

The man began to feel so hot,
he took off his coat
and sat down in a shady spot.

The Wind returned and said to the Sun,
"I huffed and I puffed
and I blew to the brim
but I could not force
the man's coat from him. . .
I can't imagine that you
were able to either!"

The Wind stopped howling long enough to look down.
There was the man, sitting under a tree.
Lo and behold!
His coat was folded up like a pillow under his head.

"How did you FORCE him to take off his coat!?"
the Wind asked in amazement.

The Sun replied,
"I did not force him at all. I lit the day!
Through gentleness I won my way."

"There MUST have been a TRICK!"
grumbled the Wind.

"It's not a trick," said the Sun.
"It's a choice and a skill.
Would you like me to show you?"

The Sun just smiled . . .

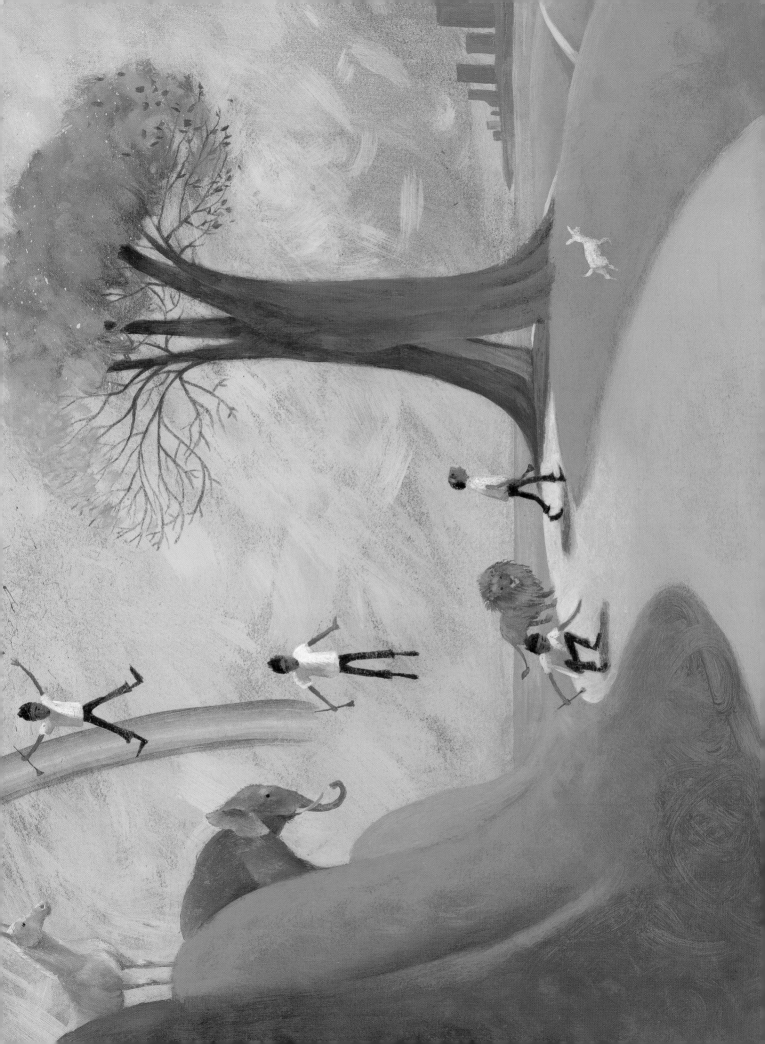

Author's Note

The Contest Between the Sun and the Wind is based on a fable attributed to a Greek slave named Aesop who lived 2,500 years ago. Passed on through the oral tradition by generations of storytellers, this metaphorical plot raises a ponderous question: *Can gentleness, instead of force, be an effective way to achieve a goal?*